TINY TOON Adventures

HAPPY BIRTHDAY, BABS!

Written by Linda Aber
Illustrated by John Costanza

A GOLDEN BOOK • NEW YORK
Western Publishing Company, Inc., Racine, Wisconsin 53404

© 1990 Warner Bros. Inc. All rights reserved. Printed in the U.S.A. No part of this book may be reproduced or copied in any form without written permission from the publisher. Tiny Toon Adventures, the Tiny Toon Adventures character names and likenesses are trademarks of Warner Bros. Inc. © 1990 Warner Bros. Inc. Looney Tunes, the Looney Tunes character names, likenesses and slogans are trademarks of Warner Bros. Inc. © 1990 Warner Bros. Inc. All other trademarks are the property of Western Publishing Company, Inc. Library of Congress Catalog Card Number: 89-82148   ISBN: 0-307-00096-6   MCMXCII

"I look mahhhhvelous!" said Babs Bunny to her reflection in the mirror. "If I half close my eyes, I can almost see myself looking like a real-life princess in this dress."

It was a special dress for a very special day. "Happy birthday, Babs! I am ready to party!" she told the mirror.

Babs had her day all planned. She would see all of her friends so they could wish her a happy birthday.

Babs took one last look in the mirror. She fluffed out her ears and smoothed down her dress. Now Babs Bunny was ready to start receiving those birthday greetings.

Babs smiled her birthday smile as she walked through Acme Acres. Soon she saw her good friend Buster Bunny.

"Hi, Buster," she called out. Buster had his head down in the grass. He was using his big teeth to mow the lawn. Buster was the fastest grass-cutter in Acme Acres.

"Can't talk right now, Babs," said Buster between bites. "I still have two more lawns to do before school. I've got to keep working to earn some money."

"That Buster," thought Babs. "All he thinks about is earning money. He's even too busy to wish me a happy birthday." Babs walked on and hoped she would see another friend soon.

Not far off, Babs saw Hamton. He was wearing
an apron. Egg yolks dripped from his chef hat. He
stood by a table covered with mixing bowls, sugar,
and all kinds of baking utensils.

"Hi, Hamton," called Babs.

Hamton didn't seem to hear her. He looked
worried as he licked a dripping beater. "If this
doesn't cook up right," he said to himself, "I'll just
have to eat it and make another one."

Babs could see that Hamton was too busy to
stop and say "Happy birthday, Babs." She walked
on sadly.

Poor Babs! Her birthday plans weren't working out the way she had hoped at all. "Some birthday," she said as she sat down on an empty bench. "Birthdays are supposed to be happy. But so far everybody seems to be too busy even to notice me."

But then Babs stopped. She stood, held her head high, and said, "Chin up, Babs! The show must go on!"

Babs fussed a little with her ears and made sure
they looked perky. She fluffed up her pretty party
dress and continued on her way. "There's sure to
be someone who has time to say 'Happy birthday,
Babs,'" she thought. She looked ahead and saw
some movement. Babs hurried to see who was
causing it.

It was Plucky Duck, who was very busy flying. He was practicing taking off and landing. Babs could see that Plucky was very good at taking off.

But he was not so good at landing. Babs stood
and watched as Plucky came crashing down into a
big green hedge.

"Nice try, Plucky," she called out. "Are you all
right?"

Plucky Duck did not answer. He rested, beak
first, in the bush. Plucky did not say "Happy
birthday, Babs." He did not say anything. So Babs
walked on.

Just when Babs was starting to feel unhappy
again, she noticed another friend. Shirley the Loon
was sitting above the ground and staring into the
crystal ball that floated in front of her.

"Hi, Shirley," Babs said. "What's happening?"

Shirley answered in a dreamlike voice, "What matters is not what is happening now, but what will be happening in the future! Ohmmmmm." Then Shirley closed her eyes and seemed to fall asleep.

Babs didn't need a crystal ball to tell her that Shirley was not even thinking about saying "Happy birthday, Babs."

"Bye, Shirley," said Babs sadly.

"What a day," Babs sighed. "What a life! I've got my birthday dress and my birthday smile, and not a friend in all of Acme Acres!"

It was a sad Babs Bunny who walked into school that day.

Everybody was already seated when Babs arrived at her class. Bugs Bunny was about to begin the day's lesson.

"Today," he said, "we will learn about how to be funny!"

"Oh, no," thought Babs. "I don't feel funny today." She took her seat behind Buster Bunny and sat quietly.

"Class," Bugs Bunny said as he climbed up on his desk, "to be funny, or not to be funny? That is the question!

"Well, my feathered, furry, and hairy friends, the answer to that question is always yes, be funny! At all costs, be funny! Spare no expense. Be funny! Funny is everything. Funny is anything! Funny is funny!"

Then he jumped off the desk. He leaned right into Babs Bunny's face and said, "There is no greater gift than the gift of laughter."

When Babs heard her teacher say the word *gift*, she felt worse than ever. It reminded her that no one had even said "Happy birthday, Babs" on this special day.

Then Babs had an idea. "I'll just have to have a party for myself," she thought. Everyone Babs wanted to invite was right there in the classroom. After class she told them all about it.

"I've decided to have a special party today,"
Babs informed her friends. "Will you come?" she
asked Buster Bunny, Hamton, Shirley the Loon,
and Plucky Duck.

"I can't," said Buster. "I'm going to another
party."

"I can't," said Hamton. "I'm also going to
another party."

"Me, too," said Plucky Duck.

"Same here," said Shirley.

Now Babs was sadder than ever. No one seemed to know that this day was an important one for her. How could all of her best friends forget her birthday? And why wasn't she invited to the party everyone else was going to?

"Hey, Babs," said Buster. "I have a great idea. Since we are all going to a party already, why don't you call off your party and come with us?"

Babs thought for a minute. She felt a little better now that she was invited to the party, too. "I guess any party is better than no party," she said, and she agreed to meet Buster at his house at three o'clock.

Babs arrived at Buster's house exactly at three o'clock. She could see that all of her friends were already there. Then Babs had the biggest surprise ever.

"Happy birthday, Babs!" they shouted. Plucky Duck flew around carrying a birthday banner. He had practiced all morning and didn't crash once.

Hamton held out a perfect birthday cake.

Shirley the Loon had gotten the news of Bab's birthday when she looked into her crystal ball. She handed Babs a birthday crystal of her own.

"Happy birthday, Babs!" said Buster, who had mowed many lawns to earn the money for the party.

"This is the happiest birthday I've ever had,"
Babs told her friends. "I knew you wouldn't
forget." Soon all of them were laughing. Babs
laughed harder than anyone. As she looked around
the room she remembered what Bugs Bunny had
said: "There is no greater gift than the gift of
laughter."

"And there's no one I'd rather be laughing with
than my friends from Acme Acres," thought Babs
as she gave each one of them her best birthday hug!